Words to Know Before You Read

shark
shells
shiny
ship
shoe
shore
shorts
shouts
shovel

www.rourkeeducationalmedia.com

Edited by Precious McKenzie
Illustrated by Ed Myer
Art Direction, Cover and Page Layout by Tara Raymo

Library of Congress PCN Data

A Ship and Shells / Meg Greve
ISBN 978-1-62169-267-6 (hard cover) (alk. paper)
ISBN 978-1-62169-225-6 (soft cover)
Library of Congress Control Number: 2012952772

Rourke Educational Media
Printed in the United States of America,
North Mankato, Minnesota

rourkeeducationalmedia.com
customerservice@rourkeeducationalmedia.com • PO Box 643328 Vero Beach, Florida 32964

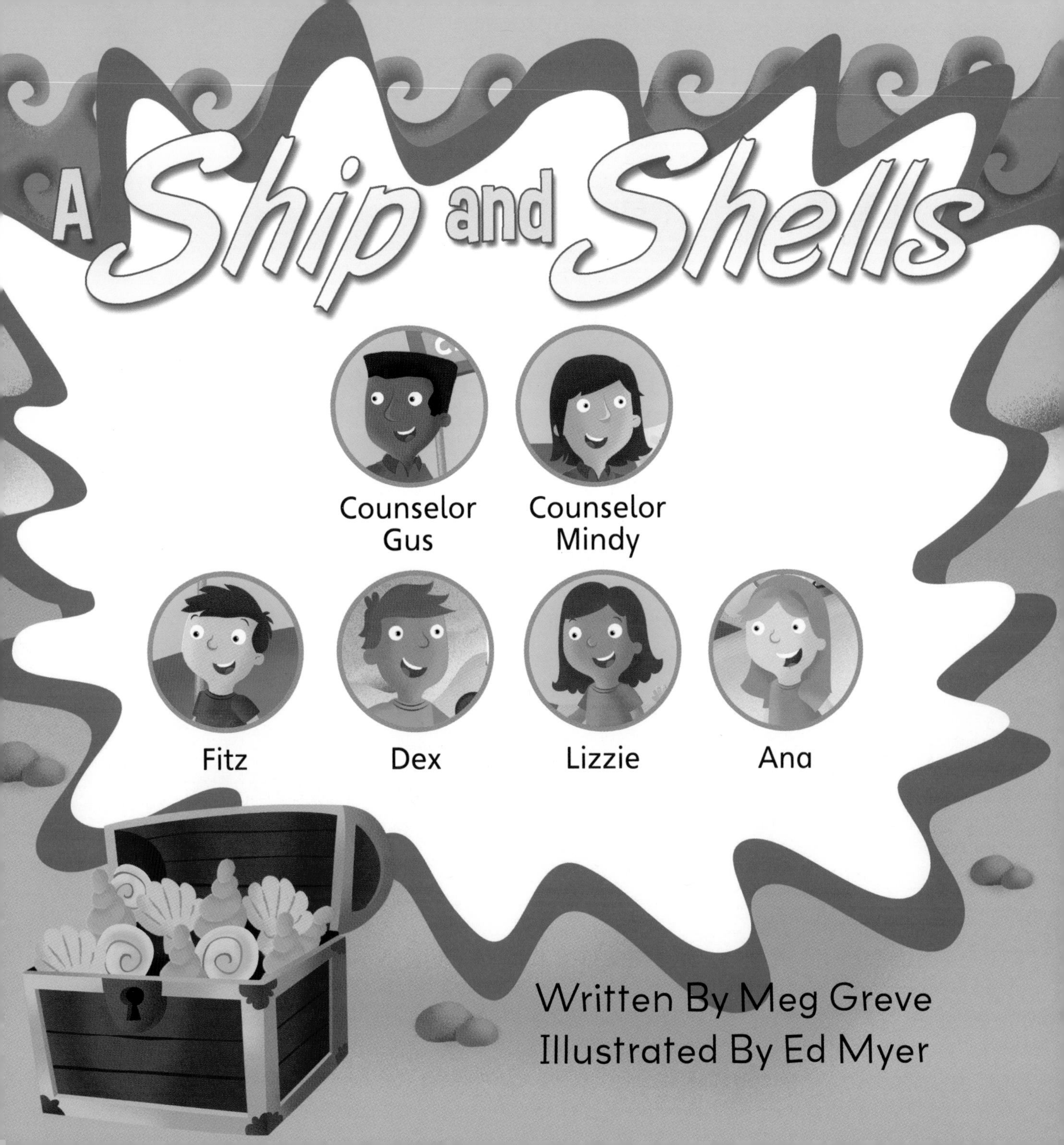
A Ship and Shells
Counselor
Gus
Counselor
Mindy
Fitz
Dex
Lizzie
Ana
Written By Meg Greve
Illustrated By Ed Myer

“Shhh,” whispers Counselor Gus.

“What are you doing?” asks Lizzie.

“I am reading a super, secret treasure map,” says Counselor Gus.

“A treasure map!” shouts Fitz.

CAMP ADVENTURE

"Look at the map. It shows we should start looking near the shore," says Counselor Mindy.

"Shhh, it's a secret!" shushes Lizzie.

"Let's go!" says Counselor Gus.

CAMP ADVENTURE

A ship is waiting near the shore.
The children climb on for a ride.

"Will I see a shark?" shudders Ana.

"I need some swim shorts,"
says Fitz.

ADVENTURE

“We are here to look for treasure. Now we need a shovel,” sighs Fitz.

“Let’s go fishing instead,” says Dex.

Dex and Fitz get a fishing pole.

Dex's pole shakes and shivers.

"We got a fish!" yells Fitz.

They pull and pull until it flops on the shore.

Is it a fish?

"It's a shoe!" giggles Ana.

She shows them the map, "Now, let's find the treasure."

"Back on board!" she shouts.

The ship soon stops on a new shore. The children share the shovels. They dig and dig.

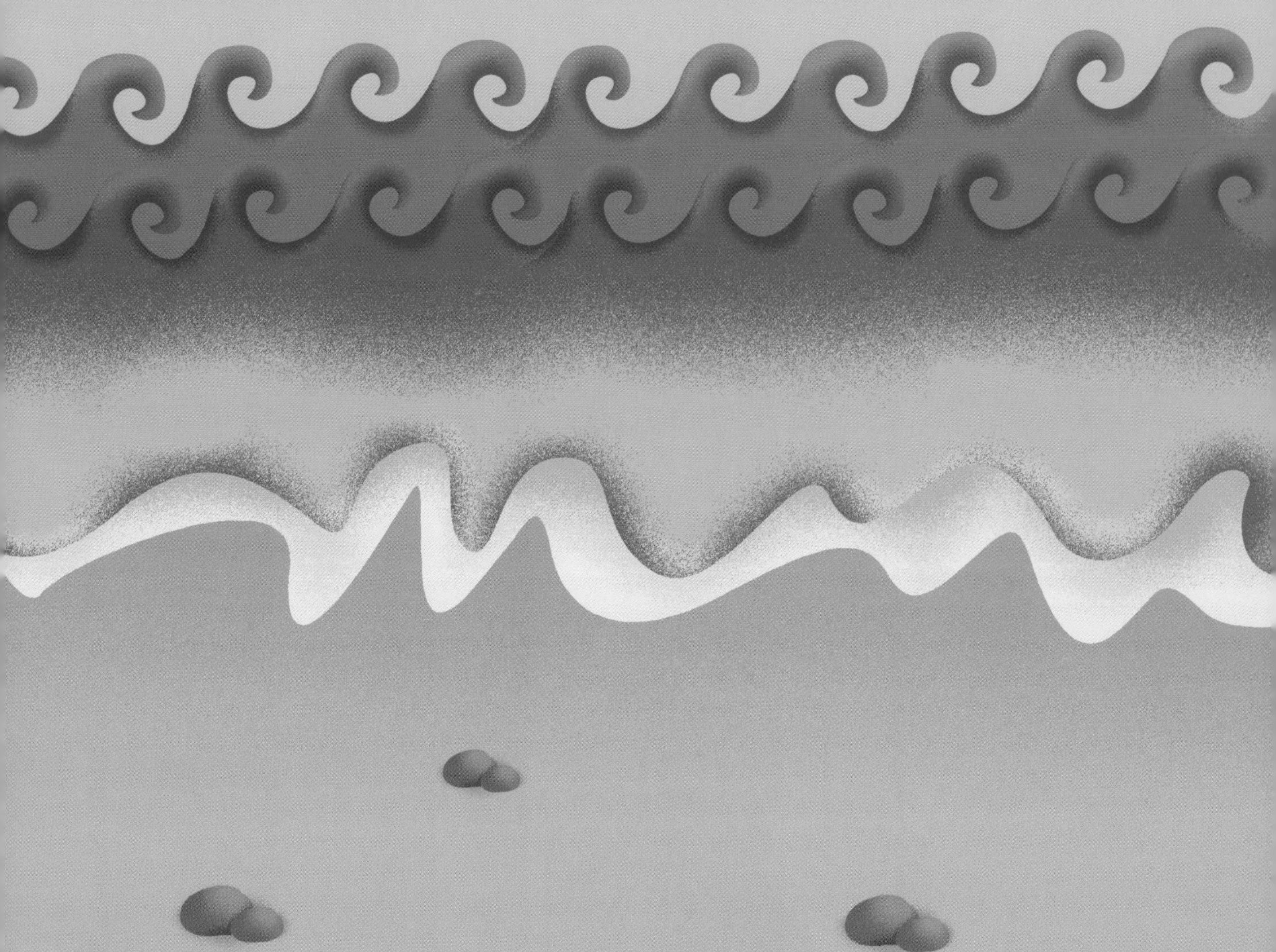

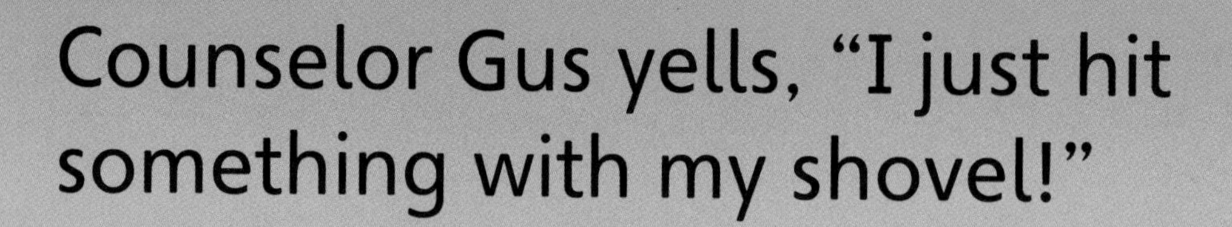

Counselor Gus yells, “I just hit something with my shovel!”

“Is it the secret treasure?” asks Ana.

“We all have to share it,” says Lizzie.

Gus and Mindy pull up the big chest.

Fitz opens the chest and peeks in.
"Oh no! It isn't shiny gold!" he cries.

"It's just a bunch of shells," says Ana.

"Let's share them anyway," says Dex.

After Reading Word Study

Picture Glossary

Directions: Look at each picture and read the definition. Write a list of all of the words you know that start with the same sound as *ship*. Remember to look in the book for more words.

shark (SHARK): A shark is a type of fish that has cartilage, gills, and usually sharp teeth.

shells (SHELZ): Shells are hard, rock-like things found in the ocean.

ship (SHIP): A ship is a large vessel that floats on the water.

shoe (SHOO): A shoe is something you wear to cover and protect your foot.

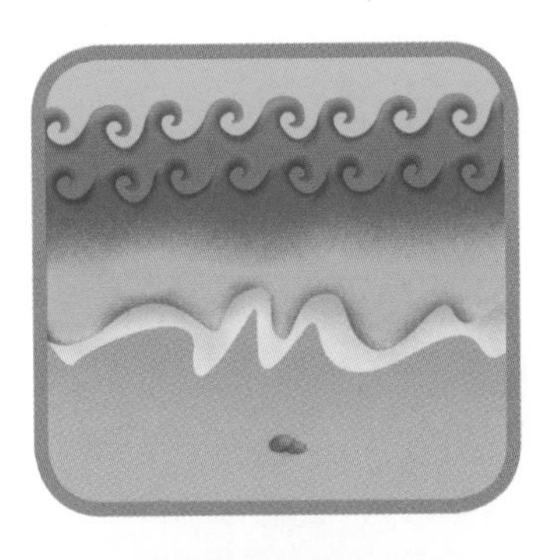

shore (SHOR): A shore is the coastline near the water.

shorts (SHORTSS): Shorts are pants that people wear. Shorts usually stop at the knees.

About the Author

Meg Greve lives in Chicago with her husband and her two kids named Madison and William. She went fishing with her kids, but didn't catch any shoes!

About the Illustrator

Ed Myer is a Manchester-born illustrator now living in London. After growing up in an artistic household, Ed studied ceramics at university but always continued drawing pictures. As well as illustration, Ed likes traveling, playing computer games, and walking little Ted (his Jack Russell).